MR. NOBODY

by Roger H...

illustrated by Roger Hargrea... ...Hargreaves

PSS!
PRICE STERN SLOAN
An Imprint of Penguin Group (USA) Inc.

Hello!

Meet Mr. Happy. Happy by name, and happy by nature.

And now, I'm going to tell you a story.

Actually, this story isn't about Mr. Happy.

Well, not really.

It's about somebody he met not very long ago. Last month, in fact.

Mr. Happy had been to tea with Little Miss Sunshine.

He thought about catching a bus to take him home. But, as it was such a nice day, he thought again, and decided to walk.

And he was glad he did!

Would you like to know why?

I shan't tell you!

Not yet, anyway.

Mr. Happy was whistling to himself as he walked along when he heard a noise.

He stopped.

There it was again!

A sort of sniffing noise.

SNIFF! SNIFF! SNIFF!

Suddenly, a drop of rain splashed on top of his head.

"That's odd," he thought to himself, looking up. "There isn't a cloud in the sky!"

And then—he couldn't believe his eyes.

You'll never guess what Mr. Happy saw.

There, sitting on the branch of a tree, was somebody who sort of was, but wasn't!

I know it sounds ridiculous, but it's true.

You could see through him!

And he was crying real big fat wet tears.

Which, of course, were what had splashed on top of Mr. Happy's head.

"Who," Mr. Happy managed to splutter, "are you?"

The person who sort of was, but wasn't, looked mournfully down at him, and in a mournful, melancholy voice, replied, "Nobody."

"Nobody?" gasped Mr. Happy. "But everybody's somebody!"

The person who sort of was, but wasn't, sighed deeply.

"Except me," he said. And he started to cry more real big fat wet tears.

Mr. Happy scratched his head, which was getting quite wet by this time.

"Can you get down?" he wondered.

"Possibly," replied Mr. Nobody. And he climbed down out of the tree.

"Where have you come from?" asked Mr. Happy.

"Nowhere." Mr. Nobody sighed the sort of sigh that breaks your heart.

"I know I used to be somebody. But I can't remember who!" He sniffed. "Or what!" He sniffed. "Or where!" He sniffed. "Or when!" He sobbed.

Mr. Happy couldn't help but stare. It isn't often you meet somebody you can see right through!

"I think," said Mr. Happy, "that you had better come home with me."

"Why?" sobbed Mr. Nobody.

"Because," said Mr. Happy, "we must do something about you."

"There's nothing you can do about a nobody," wept the person who sort of was, but wasn't.

"Of course there is," said Mr. Happy. "Follow me!"

Eventually, they reached Mr. Happy's house and went into his living room.

Mr. Happy pointed to a chair.

"Sit yourself down," he said.

It was really quite extraordinarily extraordinary, seeing somebody who was nobody sitting in a chair.

Mr. Happy sat down, too.

And thought. Hard!

"The wizard!" cried Mr. Happy. "Of course!"

So the following morning, after no breakfast, Mr. Happy took Mr. Nobody to see the wizard.

"Ah!" remarked the wizard, after Mr. Happy had tried to explain.

"Ah!" he said again, eyeing Mr. Nobody.

Mr. Nobody just stood there, looking as glum as anyone can look.

Just try turning the corners of your mouth down as far as they will go. Go on!

Well, that's about half as glum as Mr. Nobody looked.

The wizard thought and thought.

And thought some more.

"Care for a cup of tea?" he inquired.

"Nobodys don't drink nothing," replied Mr. Nobody.

"Nobodys don't drink ANYthing," said the wizard, correcting him.

"That's right," agreed Mr. Nobody.

"Aha!" cried the wizard. "That's it!"

The wizard rushed over to his workbench and started to mix up lots of different colored liquids in a huge bottle.

They bubbled and gurgled together and let off little puffs of white smoke.

BUBBLE! BUBBLE! GURGLE! PUFF!
BUBBLE! BUBBLE! GURGLE! PUFF!

"What color would you like to be?" the wizard asked Mr. Nobody.

"Nobodys aren't colored," came the sad reply.

"You choose!" said the wizard, pointing at Mr. Happy.

Mr. Happy thought.

"Well," he said, "I've always really rather quite enjoyed being yellow."

"YELLOW IT SHALL BE!" shouted the wizard as he poured more liquid into the bottle.

Suddenly, with one huge PUFF of white smoke, the liquid turned bright yellow!

"Right!" cried the wizard. "Drink that!"

"Nobodys don't drink nothing," said Mr. Nobody.

"EXACTLY," shouted the wizard at the top of his voice. "NOBODYS DON'T DRINK NOTHING! THEREFORE, NOBODYS MUST DRINK SOMETHING!"

Mr. Nobody took hold of the bottle and took a small sip.

"MORE!" cried the wizard. "Much MORE!"

Mr. Nobody shut his eyes.

And took a deep breath.

And swallowed all of the liquid!

Mr. Happy and the wizard watched and waited, and waited and watched.

Nothing happened!

"Told you so," said Mr. Nobody.

And he sighed, another one of those sighs that break your heart.

But—wait a minute!

Did their eyes deceive them, or—

They looked at Mr. Nobody's feet.

They were turning sort of, yes, yellow!

Yes! Decidedly yellow!

Definitely yellow!

Then Mr. Nobody's legs turned yellow!

And then his body!

And then his arms!

"His nose!" Mr. Happy shouted. "What about his nose?"

They watched and they waited. And they waited and they watched.

Nothing happened!

Suddenly, Mr. Nobody sneezed!

And immediately after he sneezed, with an enormous

POP! ATISHOOPOP!

his nose turned yellow as well!

Oh, I wish you'd been there to see Mr. Nobody's face.

His mouth stopped turning down and started turning up.

And up, and up, and up again!

"Well," chuckled Mr. Happy, "I told you so—"

"Everybody's a SOMEBODY!"